A Hodgepog Book

Hodgepog Books acknowledges the ongoing support of the Canada Council for the Arts.

Editors: Luanne Armstrong and Dorothy Woodend

Cover design by Dorothy Woodend
Inside layout by Linda Uyehara Hoffman
Set in Biffo and Goudy in Quark XPress 4.1
Printed at Hignell Book Printing

A Hodgepog Book for Kids

Published in Canada by Hodgepog Books,
3476 Tupper Street
Vancouver, BC
V5Z 3B7
Telephone (604) 874-1167
Email:woodend@telus.net

National Library of Canada Cataloguing in Publication Data

Horne, Constance.
Papa's surprises

1. Frontier and pioneer life—Juvenile fiction. I. Title.
PS8565.06693P36 2002 jC813'.54 C2002-910988-4
PZ7.H67Pa 2002

Table of Contents

Phillipe and Celine Doucet always thought of the time when they were nine and eight years old, as the year of Papa's best surprises.

Papa Doucet loved to give his family a surprise. Sometimes he would secretly whittle toy cars or boats for the children. Once he brought home an old tire from Grandpère's truck and hung it from a tree for a swing. Once he rowed Mama a long way down the stream to see an avocet bird on its nest. The children were not allowed to go because they might scare it away. The avocet is a very shy bird. Humans seldom see it. Mama's eyes were shining when she described the graceful brown bird.

Whenever there was a new baby in the family, Papa would tell the children that their mother had gone away to bring them a surprise. Even he was surprised when she brought home the twins, Armand and Albertine. Since then there had been Louisa and Robert. With Emmanuel, the big brother, there were now seven children in the Doucet family.

There was no new baby in 1934, just Papa's two wonderful gifts, one in Winter and one in Spring.

Section One
A Gift From Heaven

CHAPTER ONE

An hour after sunrise, the Doucet homestead in the Interlake District of Manitoba was muffled in a white and silent world. Snow had begun falling the night before. It was still coming down in large, soft flakes. Gently, it built up fluffy white comforters on the roofs of the house and outbuildings. It smoothed out all the humps and bumps on the ground. It decorated the bare limbs of the birch and aspen trees with white lace.

From behind one of these trees, a wolverine stepped noiselessly onto the edge of the clearing. He paused and crouched low. His white-tipped ears twitched while his yellow eyes stared unblinking into the falling snow. The only sound was a plop as a blob of snow fell from an overloaded branch. Ahead loomed the shape of a building. The wolverine padded toward it.

He had been here before. That time, he had found a small hole. He had made it bigger with his strong teeth and sharp claws. Once inside the building, he had ripped open sacks of food stored on the shelves for the winter. He was searching for the dead animals whose scent still clung to the dried pelts hanging on the walls.

Now, he tramped around the building, pausing often

to scrape at the rough boards with his claws. By the time he reached his starting point, his footprints had filled in with new snow. He found no opening. Just as he bared his teeth to snarl, he heard a click and a soft scraping sound. In a moment he was back among the trees, heading for his den.

CHAPTER TWO

The sounds the wolverine heard were repeated in reverse. First, the soft scrape of a door on a wooden floor and then the tiny click of a latch. Phillipe Doucet had come quietly out of the house. Like the wolverine, he paused to listen. Not a sound. His younger brothers and sisters had not wakened. Mama was up nursing the baby, but they made no noise. He had come for an armload of wood. It was his job to build up the fire in the stove and have the kitchen warm for Mama and the children by breakfast time.

After the wolverine's first visit, the Doucets were left with only enough flour, oatmeal and sugar to last two weeks. And they had three more months of winter ahead of them. Papa made the shed animal-proof. Then he set out on the long trek to town to replace the ruined food. He took Emmanuel with him. Phillipe, nine years old, was the man of the house while they were away.

This was the fourth day since they left. Phillipe looked toward the south. On a clear day in winter, when the trees were bare, the Doucets could see past the frozen creek and across the flat landscape to their grandparents' home three kilometers away. Today, Phillipe could not see three meters through the curtain of snow. It was a good thing that Papa had taken the big work toboggan and two pairs of snowshoes. This new-fallen snow would make walking and hauling very difficult.

Phillipe tramped the few steps to the woodpile, excited to be the first to make footprints in the new snow. When he brushed off the woodpile's white cap, the falling flakes swirled in a silent dance. With his arms full of wood, he walked backwards in his own footsteps. Yesterday, he had read a story about a pirate who did that in the sand of a desert island. The pirate wanted to fool the enemies who would try to find his buried treasure Phillipe thought that was very smart.

As Phillipe reached the door, he heard the faint sound of someone breathing. It came from outside the house. He strained to see as far as the creek, but the moving snow played tricks on his eyes. The sound came again. Someone was panting heavily. A form began to emerge out of the white. It was a man on snowshoes, bent forward with his hands up to his right shoulder. A smaller form behind him was also tugging at something.

Phillipe banged loudly on the door with the butt ends of the logs he was carrying.

"They're here! They're here! Papa and Emmanuel are home!" he yelled.

The door was flung open and Mama stood behind Phillipe with baby Robert in her arms. Celine, still in her nightgown and with bare feet, ran up beside her.

"Papa! Papa!" she shouted.

Mama sent her back to put on socks and a sweater.

Her place was taken by the twins, Armand and Albertine. They had dragged a quilt with them and wrapped it around themselves and stood on its trailing corners.

"Allo, Papa! Allo Manny!" they called over and over at the top of their voices.

From the bedroom, little sister Louisa was shouting, "Me see! Me see!"

Celine came back with the little girl in her arms. They added their voices to the noise.

While all this was going on, the two figures came slowly closer. They called back greetings to the group in the doorway but used most of their breath and strength for the final pull to the house. Now the children could all see the load on the toboggan.

Except for the cooing baby, the family stood silent as they stared in astonishment.

The sacks of food that Papa had gone to buy were piled on top of one another at the front of the sled. Even under the blanket of snow, they all recognized those. But the whole of the rest of the toboggan was taken up by a huge packing case.

After a long moment of staring, Celine asked, "What is it, Papa?"

"A surprise," he answered, laughing. "Move back, now. Vite! Vite! We must get it inside where it can warm up."

CHAPTER THREE

Papa and Emmanuel took off their snowshoes and stuck them upright in a drift. While Phillipe dumped his load in the wood box and hurried out again, Mama put Robert in the cradle and sent the rest of them to get clothes on. From the bedroom where she was dressing Louisa and helping the twins with buttons and boot laces, Celine heard Phillipe laughing.

"It won't go through the door, Papa," he said.

"It will go through on the skinny side," Papa answered.

"It isn't skinny anywhere," said Phillipe.

"You'll see," said Papa. "Come and help us push."

Celine followed the twins back to the doorway. The toboggan had been backed up so that it rested on the door sill. The part of the crate that Celine could see was as tall as she was. Sideways, it fitted the doorway with just centimeters to spare on each side. She peeked through the cracks and saw Manny and Phillipe holding the box while Papa pulled the sled away. Manny pressed on the top of the box to keep it from tilting into the snow.

"Heave!" called Papa. "Heave! Heave!"

The crate inched inward. Celine and Mama put their shoulders to the boards on either side and helped to push. It was heavy!

At last, it was inside.

"Whew!" said Papa, "That was a job! I'll put those sacks away. Don't try to move the crate without me."

Manny leaned on the closed door and beat his mittens against his pant leg to dislodge the snow. He grinned at the twins who were jumping up and down.

"What's in it, Manny?" they yelled.

"A surprise," he answered.

"Tell us! Tell us!"

Their big brother shook his head.

Celine grabbed the broom and swept off the top and sides of the box to uncover the printing.

T. EATON COMPANY
MAIL ORDER HOUSE

Even Albertine and Armand could read that. Eaton's catalogue was their favourite picture book. At least once a year, sometimes twice, Mama would fill in the order form. A few weeks later, a big box would arrive. It might contain new shoes for Mama or Celine or boots for Papa or material to make dresses and shirts or a blanket or a new kettle or any number of things. Always, there was a bag of candies. The twins had never seen a parcel as big as this one!

Celine had. When she was about as old as Armand and Albertine, the rocking chair had come in a big crate from Eaton's. She looked at her mother. Mama's eyes were wide and one hand covered her mouth. Celine followed her gaze to the printing in one corner of the box.

"What's that mean, Mama?" asked Celine.

Mama snapped out of her dream and laughed.

"I don't know," she said. "It's a mystery to me, too."

She took the broom and swept the snow out the door. When she finished, her color had returned to normal but her eyes still sparkled.

"Breakfast," she said. "We must eat. Phillipe, tend the stove. Celine, set the table. Emmanuel, did you and Papa eat at Grandmama's?"

"No. Papa wanted to get home before the snow was too deep. It was hard enough work pulling that load."

"Did you pull it all the way from town?" asked Celine, astonished.

"Don't be dumb!" answered Phillipe. "They borrowed Grandpère's horse and sleigh, didn't you, Manny?"

Emmanuel nodded. "That's right. We got back to their place just at dark yesterday. When we saw how hard the snow was coming down this morning, Grandmere wanted us to stay till it stopped. But Papa wanted to see your faces when you opened the ... Oops! I nearly told!"

Just then Papa came in.

"Remember your promise, Son," he said.

"Sorry, Papa," laughed Manny. "I'll keep my mouth shut."

Armand and Albertine flew to their father and each hugged a snowy leg.

"Open it, Papa! Open it!"

"No, not yet. It has to warm up."

"When, Papa, when?"

"After supper."

Everyone protested noisily.

"Oui, after supper. I'm going to walk around the trapline today. It's been four days. I can't wait any longer."

"Well, the box can't stay there, Gabriel," said Mama. "It's in the way."

"D'accord," said Papa. He hung his jacket and hat on a peg near the door and turned to look for a place for the surprise.

The front room ran right across the width of the house. It was already very crowded. At the kitchen end there was a big cooking range, a dry sink and a cupboard for dishes. Next to the range was a large table covered with oilcloth. Celine was setting it for breakfast. Mama's sewing machine was between the two front windows. Opposite it was the door to the bedrooms with a small, round stove on one side and the rocking chair on the other. A couch and a glass-fronted bookcase took up all the space on the far wall. There was a chest under each window and an easy chair in front of the bookcase Where could the crate go?

Celine watched Papa carefully.

"Twins," he said finally, "move the rocker. That's the place for our surprise, against that wall. Come, boys, help me move it."

Now Celine was sure she knew what was in the box. Another rocking chair! Just what she had often wished for. On long winter evenings one of their favourite family games was to go on a rocking chair voyage. Papa would sit in the chair. As many children as could fit would pile in his lap. Then he'd rock hard, making the chair move across the room. Papa would think up a wonderful story about where they were going. Sometimes he said they were on a fishing boat on the lake. Sometimes the chair was a canoe and they would all sing voyageur songs as they pretended to run the rapids. Sometimes it was a truck or a train taking them to the big city.

"Not too close to the wall, boys," said Papa. "Leave room to get the box open. Just a light push now. One, two, push!"

Scrape! Scrape! Then a long sigh, a moan and a squawk that came from inside the crate.

"What was that?" gasped Albertine.

"It's alive!" whispered Armand.

"A parrot!" yelled Phillipe.

The pirate in his storybook walked around with a parrot on his shoulder. It was always saying, "Pieces of eight" or "Yo, ho, ho." Wouldn't it be fun to have a bird that could talk?

"You're crazy!" said Emmanuel. "A parrot's not much bigger than a crow, probably. Look at the size of that box."

"It's in a cage," said Phillipe.

"And how do you think it could live shut up in there with no air?"

CHAPTER FOUR

Just then Mama called them all to the table. The porridge had been simmering on the stove all night. Celine ladled it into bowls while Mama fried slices of pork. The twins kept pestering Papa to open the box before he went on the trapline, but he wouldn't agree. It would have to be after supper because the surprise had to warm up.

"Well, tell us what it is," they begged.

"A gift from heaven," answered their father with a big grin.

"I know! I know, Papa!" said Celine. "You bought it with the money from the fox skin. That's what you called it when you found the fox in the trap — a gift from heaven."

"That's just what it was," he answered. "The only silver fox I've ever caught. Do you remember its fur? Black with silver tips. What a beauty! It brought a good price."

Mama frowned down the table at him. "But, Gabriel, I had plans for that money."

"Now, now, Mama! A gift from heaven isn't meant to be used for ordinary things like boots or underwear or frying pans. It's for something special, something you'd never buy yourself, something that will bring happiness. Isn't that so, children?"

They all shouted in agreement with Papa.

"You'll like the surprise, Marietta. I promise you will," he said coaxingly.

Mama tried to keep a stern face but her eyes were shining. Finally, she smiled.

Mama packed a lunch for Papa and he set off on the trapline. The rest of them had to put in the long hours until the evening. They spent a lot of time guessing what the surprise could be. Phillipe and Armand pressed their ears to the side of the box but heard nothing.

"It's a doll house like the one in the catalogue," said Albertine.

"And cowboy boots for me," added her twin.

"What do you think it is, Louisa?" asked Celine.

The little girl had been slow to walk and talk. Even at a year and a half, she still clung to the legs of tables and chairs. She could say Mama and Papa and had a name for each of her brothers and sisters. The rest of the time she pointed at what she wanted. Now, she was grinning up at Celine who was sitting at the big table doing her school work.

"What's in the box, Louise?" asked Celine.

The little girl looked at it and then back to her sister.

"Candy!" she said.

They all laughed.

"Where did you learn that word?" asked Mama. She picked her up. "Come, let Celine get on with her arithmetic. You, too, Phillipe. The time will go faster if you put your mind on something besides the surprise."

Armand groaned. "Oh! I can't wait!"

"Of course you can," scolded his mother. "Finish your printing. You'll be starting school next summer. We want the teacher to think you're another smart Doucet."

There was a little school house on Grandpère's property, but it was only open two or three months in the summer. In winter, the weather was often too cold or snowy for the children of the district to travel two or three kilometers. Besides, no teacher wanted to spend the winter in such an isolated place. In spring and fall, the marshland was so boggy that people sank into it. So, each summer, the Department of Education sent someone to teach the dozen or so children in all grades from one to eight. Every year a different teacher came. It was always exciting to wonder who it would be.

Papa had gone to that school until he was ten years old. He had learned to read and write and do arithmetic. Emmanuel, who would be twelve next summer, thought that was a good age to quit school. He liked helping his father on the farm and trapline. Why did he need book learning for that? Today, even though it was still snowing, he was doing outside chores. It kept him away from the twins' pestering.

Celine and Phillipe both took after their mother. They liked to learn. Mama had grown up in a small town where her father owned a general store. The town school stayed open ten months of the year. She had even been to a convent school for two years. She was a good student

and the nuns loved her. They discovered her talent for music and taught her to play the piano. In her final year at the convent, she had the job of pumping the bellows of the old harmonium in the chapel while the music teacher played it. As a reward, she was sometimes allowed to perform. Once she had played when the Bishop was visiting! Afterwards, he was astonished to learn that the organist was a young girl, not a nun at all. The children loved to hear Mama tell that story. Of course, she hadn't had a chance to play very often since her marriage. The closest piano they knew about was in the hall in the village. The town church had a creaky old harmonium.

The nuns from her old school still kept in touch with Mama. They sent her used textbooks and hectographed copies of the lessons they taught. They sent scribblers and pencils and Bible text cards to give out for good work. Mama could have used more of those! She thought all her children's work was good.

CHAPTER FIVE

The noise level both inside and out went up and down throughout the long day. Inside, it was fairly quiet for the hour Celine and Phillipe worked at their lessons. After that, all sorts of sounds filled the room. When Robert was awake, he cried and cooed. Louisa's favourite toy, a wooden mallet, went tap, tap, tap on the lid of the trunk, the sides of the mysterious box and the tray of her high chair at lunch time. Stove lids rattled, the sewing machine whirred, the children talked, argued and laughed. Mama and Celine thumped the table as they kneaded the bread dough.

Outside, the snow fell steadily and silently. Emmanuel's feet made no sound as he walked to the creek. But his axe made high, ringing notes when he chopped open the hole in the ice to fill the water pails. Later, the thud of the axe chopping logs into kindling was duller and louder. When the children tumbled out of the house after lunch, the air was filled with their happy voices. They slid on the ice of the creek when Manny shovelled a path for them. They climbed on the roof of the shed and jumped into the soft snow below. They pelted one another with handfuls of snow and took turns dragging Louisa on the small toboggan. They ganged up on Emmanuel, knocked him down and sat on him, threatening to rub his face with snow unless he told them Papa's secret.

He broke free and jumped up.

"Wait and see," he said, backing away from the twins.

"Is it something to play with?" asked Albertine.

"For Mama to play," he answered.

"For Mama," groaned Armand. "Not for us?"

"Sure, it'll be fun for you too. Now stop asking me. I'm not going to tell."

When it began to get dark, they went inside and waited for supper and Papa.

At last he came and they greeted him noisily.

"How many pelts, Papa?" asked Emmanuel over the din.

"Two good muskrats," he answered. "One other was ruined by le carcajou! That devil!"

"The wolverine again," exclaimed Mama in fear. "Can he get at the food?"

"Not this time," said Papa grimly. He pulled out his chair and sat in front of a plateful of steaming stew. "The shed is safe. I made sure of that."

When everyone was seated there was a moment of absolute silence while Mama waited for every head to bow. Then she said grace.

"Amen," said Papa at the end. "Well, now, who has figured out what is in the crate?"

They all told their guesses. A parrot in a cage, a rocking chair, a doll house, cowboy boots, a stove for the bedrooms, books, a washing machine for Mama, new clothes for everyone.

Louisa banged her spoon to the rhythm of the voices.

"Candy!" she shouted into a lull.

Papa roared with laughter.

"Now, Mama, how about you? Have you guessed?" he asked.

She shook her head but Celine saw the crinkle of a smile at the corner of her mouth.

Celine was too excited to eat. She cleaned her plate because that was the rule, but she couldn't understand how Papa and the boys could take time to eat second helpings.

At last, Papa pushed back his chair.

"Well, you children have waited long enough. Let's open the surprise," he said. "Leave the dishes, Mama. We'll clean up later. Phillipe, fetch me the crow bar. Now, stand back, twins. Give me room. Manny, come and help."

Papa took off the top of the crate first. No one but Mama was tall enough to see in. Armand and Albertine climbed on a kitchen chair but all they saw was a long bag full of packing shavings.

Albertine muttered, "Hurry up! Hurry up!" over and over. Armand moaned and clutched his stomach. Celine knew exactly how he felt. She was almost sick with excitement herself. She tried to peek past Papa and her big brother as they worked at the back of the case. She helped to pull away more bags of packing while Phillipe hauled the back panel to one side.

"Now for the front," said Papa.

"Hurray! Hurray!" yelled the twins.

They jumped down and crowded against Celine and Phillipe. Mama, holding Louisa, stood close behind them.

At the first screech of a nail pulling loose, they all held their breath. In complete silence they listened to seven more screeches. Then came the scraping of the casing being pushed aside and the plop, plop, plop of packing bags dropping to the floor. At last they could see the surprise!

It was a piece of furniture made of polished wood. Sticking out from the middle were two rows of white and black keys. They looked like teeth. Above them was a red cloth held in place by wooden slats. Just below the keys hung two wooden boards, like paddles. Down at the bottom, parallel to the floor, were more boards.

Mama gasped. Celine looked up at her Her eyes were shining above her pink cheeks.

"Oh, Gabriel," she breathed.

"What is it?" asked Armand in bewilderment.

"It's a harmonium," answered Celine. "For Mama."

"For all of us," boomed Papa. "Mama will play music for all of us."

CHAPTER SIX

Half an hour later, Mama sat on a chair on front of the keyboard. The book, *Sacred Songs*, was propped on the music rack. It was one of the three books that Celine had found in a parcel tucked in the packing case. The others were a book of folk songs and one of popular tunes. Mama decided to begin with the first hymn she had ever played in chapel—"Angels We Have Heard On High".

Celine was disappointed to discover that there were no bellows to pump. The minute she saw it, she had decided to learn to play this instrument. It would have been fun to start by pumping for Mama the way Mama herself did for the nuns. But Papa explained that this was an improved version of the harmonium. The player made the air flow by working the lowest pedals with her feet.

He was sitting in the rocking chair with Louisa on his left knee and Robert in the crook of his right arm. Emmanuel, Phillipe and Celine stood behind their mother. Armand and Albertine squatted on each side of her watching her feet.

She pressed down a few times. There was a soft moaning sound like they had heard earlier that morning.

"Is that all it does?" asked Armand.

Mama pressed down a key. Squawawawk!

Armand fell on his rump in surprise.

When they had all stopped laughing at him,

Emmanuel said, "Play the song, Mama."

"It's been so long," she answered. "I don't know if I can."

"Sure you can!" boomed Papa. "Play!"

Her hands moved nervously over the keys, barely touching them.

"Try, Mama," coaxed Celine.

"I will," said Mama. "But don't expect too much. Remember, I haven't played in years."

Peep. Peep. Peep Peep. Blat!

"Oops," said Mama.

She tried again.

Peep, peep, peep, peep, PEEP, pip, peep.

At the end of the piece she was pressing the keys down firmly.

"Bravo!" said Papa.

The children echoed him.

Smiling, Mama looked through one of the other books.

"Here's one I know—'A la claire fontaine'."

Papa sang the words he remembered and hummed the rest.

"Is there one the children know?" he asked.

Celine and Phillipe leaned over and turned the pages of the song book. Together they shouted, "En roulant ma boule!"

Mama played the first notes and they all began to sing.

Mama threw up her hands. "No, no, no," she said. "You must sing the same notes that I play. Listen." She played a few bars. "Now try."

They did.

"Celine has it," she said. "And Papa. Phillipe is not bad. Listen carefully, twins. We'll try again."

This time they sang it through to the end, even though they didn't all stay in tune all the time.

Next they sang "Allouette". Papa roared out the solo lines and the rest of them joined in the chorus and did the actions. Mama had to press the loud lever with her left knee to make the organ sound above their voices. She played several more tunes. Sometimes they sang along, sometimes they just listened. Then Mama played a march. Emmanuel grabbed the broom, sloped it over his shoulder and high-stepped back across the room. Louisa slipped off Papa's knee and marched behind him. The rest of them fell into line.

TRAMP! TRAMP! TRAMP! TRAMP!

They marched round and round the room, zig-zagging among the furniture. They stamped their feet hard. They laughed and shouted. From his chair, Papa called out, "Hup! Hup! Hup!" Mama had the loud pedal on full.

Suddenly, baby Robert let out a bellow that rose above the uproar.

Mama stopped playing. The marchers stood still.

"Oh, ho," said Papa. "This one will be a singer. Such

lungs!"

He put the baby up on his shoulder and patted his back. The roaring went on.

"Oh, poor babe!" said Mama. "We've frightened him with our noise. What are we thinking of? It's way past bedtime for all of us."

Celine and Albertine stood behind Papa, patting Robert's head and making soothing noises. The roars became screams.

"Play a lullaby, Marietta," said Papa. "Vite! Before I go deaf."

Mama played softly. The screams became sobs and then whimpers. Papa cradled Robert in his arms and rocked gently. Finally, the soft music was louder than the baby's tiny hiccoughs. No one else made a sound until his eyelids closed and he slept.

Quietly, Mama took him from Papa's arms and carried him into the bedroom. Celine took Louisa's hand and tiptoed after her. She tucked her into bed. Then she helped the twins into their night clothes before climbing in beside Louisa.

It had been a long, exciting day. In a very few minutes all the children except Phillipe were asleep. He lay in bed listening to Mama and Papa talk quietly as they tidied the kitchen and banked the stoves for the night. He heard Mama's voice as if from a long way off.

"Thank you, Gabriel. It's truly a gift from heaven to

be able to play music again."

Phillipe fell asleep with a smile on his face. Soon the only sound inside the house was the quiet breathing of nine sleepers.

CHAPTER SEVEN

Outside, the wolverine lurked at the edge of the woods. Unseen by Gabriel, he had followed the man home and watched him put the muskrats in the shed. For hours he had waited and watched the noisy house. He waited still, even after the light went out and all sounds ceased.

At last, he moved cautiously to the edge of the clearing. He crouched, white-tipped ears alert and yellow eyes scanning the whole scene. Only a few flakes drifted down. Although it was long past sundown, it was easy to see the dark buildings nestled in the white snow.

Once more, the wolverine headed for the storage shed. This time, his legs sank deep into the powdery snow and the fur of his belly swept a path between his paw prints. Once more, he circled the building and failed to find an opening. At the end of the circuit he gave a muffled snarl

of rage. He listened. All was silent. Again he went around the shed, pausing to attack the boards with his claws. This scratching noise was the only sound in the silent landscape. Back where he began, he uttered a loud, fierce growl. It shattered the peace of the night and startled even the wolverine. He bounded back to the woods.

Both Papa and Phillipe half awoke at the sound. Then they dropped back to sleep. A thin wisp of smoke rising from the chimney was the only movement until fresh snow began to fall from the black sky.

Soon the animal's tracks were filled in. The Doucet homestead slept peacefully and quietly under its soft, white blanket.

Section Two
Spring Adventure

CHAPTER ONE

Celine Doucet's rubber boots squish-sqashed through the swampy ground as she carried the water pail to the stream. After filling the pail, she set it down on a tuft of old marsh grass. The water was so cold that it made her hands numb She rubbed them hard to warm them. Along the stream she could see pockets of ice in places sheltered from the sun. Everywhere else the snow had melted. The slightly higher ground around the house was dry but the fields were covered with water. She smiled as the tiny ripples made by the wind sparkled in the sunshine. Between them, the sun and wind would dry up the fields. She sighed as she looked across the stream to her grandparents' farm. It would be weeks before they could cross that bog except by rowboat.

Suddenly she heard a wonderful sound. HONK! HONK! HONK!

She looked up. A long vee of geese was flying north. Celine shouted with joy. "Hello, geese! Hello, geese!"

The whole family tumbled out of doors. Papa, Emmanuel and Philipe came from the shed, Mama and the other children from the house. They all gazed upward and smiled at the birds.

"Spring at last," said Mama.

In the next few days, the air was filled with honks, quacks, screeches and whistles as thousands of birds flew over the homestead. Hundreds of them settled close by to build nests and raise families. There were many kinds of ducks, some gulls and even a few great blue herons. The herons were Phillipe's favorites. They seemed like the kind of bird a pirate might see on an island in the ocean. Celine and Albertine liked the ducks which would soon have fluffy babies following them in a line.

As the ducklings grew, the land would dry out. Papa would plow the three fields, one for vegetables, one for oats and the big one for wheat. Then it would be time for school. Before the snow melted, Grandmere had written to the Department of Education in Winnipeg to tell them that there were seven Doucet children ready to go to school. There was her own youngest son Pierre who was eleven, her second son"s four children, Celine, Phillipe, Armand and Albertine and her fifth son's two, Marie Angela and Jean.

Now they were all waiting anxiously for a reply to the letter. Who would the teacher be this year? Celine played school with the twins. She taught them to print the letters and the numbers and their names. She wanted to be proud of them in front of the teacher and their cousins.

Every spring when the fields dried out they were covered with stones. Some were as small as a duck's egg, some

as big as a teakettle. All had to be lifted by hand and carried to the edges of the fields. That was the children's job. They hated it. Stooping, lifting and carrying all day was hard work.

"We cleaned this field last year," said Armand with a groan. "Where do the stones come from?"

Phillipe dropped a heavy rock on to the pile and rubbed his back with his right hand. With his left hand he waved at the fields. "All the land around here is made up of soil and stones," he said. "When the water sinks into the earth, the stones float to the top."

"Why can't they sink to the bottom," muttered Armand as he plodded after his brother back to the middle of the field.

Some days later, when Celine put down the very last rock, she stopped to examine the wild rose bushes that grew all along the stone fence. Tiny green leaves already covered the yellow stems of the bushes. At the ends of some twigs she saw tight red buds. Soon the fields would be bordered with sweet smelling pink roses. If the new teacher was a woman, Celine would pick a big bunch for her on the first day of school.

Papa walked over to Grandpère's place to borrow the horse so that he could plow the fields. There were no leaves on the trees yet. The family could watch his return from a long way off. They spied saddlebags on the horse. What was in them?

There was a parcel for Mama from the nuns with music books for the harmonium and story books for the children. But Papa also brought exciting news. The government was sending a teacher. They told Grandmere to get the school house ready and they would send a message when Grandpère should meet the train in town.

"Is the teacher a man or a lady?" asked Celine.

"A man," answered Papa. "M. Henri Lafitte."

Phillipe shouted. "That's the name of a pirate in my book," he said. "Is he a pirate?"

Celine laughed at him. "There aren't any pirates any more. He's a teacher."

The children had a day off while Papa plowed the vegetable garden and then it was back to work. Celine and Phillipe helped Emmanuel plant potatoes. More stooping and bending. The twins helped Mama plant peas, beans, beets and turnips. Papa and the horse plowed the other fields. When all the work was done everyone was very, very tired.

At supper time Papa looked around the table.

"Well," he said, "I'm proud of you all. You've worked hard. Now you can have a holiday until school opens."

"When will that be?" asked Celine.

"Soon," answered Papa. "I'll find out exactly when I take the horse back tomorrow."

CHAPTER TWO

Papa was gone all day. Celine kept busy sorting out all the lessons she and Phillipe had done with Mama and adding the best of Armand and Albertine's work to the pile.

Phillipe tried to play pirates in the rowboat with the twins but Albertine was very reluctant to wield a sword, even a pretend one. The rowboat was a slow, clumsy craft, nothing like a sleek sailing ship. They tied it up to the stake on the bank of the stream and waited for Papa to come back with news about school. But by the time he returned, they were all asleep in bed.

Next morning at breakfast, Celine saw that Papa had the twinkle in his eye that meant good news.

"Is it soon, Papa?" she asked. "Does school start soon?"

He nodded. "Oui, oui."

"When? When?" demanded Phillipe and Albertine and Armand.

"Three more days. M. Lafitte will arrive on Saturday and school will start Monday morning."

"Not till Monday," moaned Celine.

"Ah, but I have a surprise for you," said Papa. "I brought it home last night."

"A surprise, Papa? Like the harmonium?" asked Celine.

"Non. Not like the harmonium, but still a nice surprise."

Armand pushed back his chair and walked around the room.

"Where is it?" he asked.

Albertine and Phillipe joined Armand in searching. They could see nothing new in the room.

"Is it as big as the harmonium?" asked Phillipe.

"Well now," said Papa, "I guess it's as big if you squished down the harmonium and stretched it out."

Celine laughed. "Squished it down and stretched it out? Is it a table?"

"Not a table," answered Papa with a grin.

"A sofa?" asked Phillipe.

"Not a sofa."

"Can we play with it?" asked Armand.

"You can play in it," said Papa.

"Only if you are very, very careful," said Mama. "You must promise to be very, very careful."

"What is it, Mama?"

"Where is it, Papa?"

Papa stood up and strode to the door.

The family paraded to the stream. Papa was in front with the twins dancing around him asking, "What is it? What is it?" Next came Emmanuel and Phillipe. Then Celine, carrying Louise, and after them Mama with Robert.

"I see it! I see it!" yelled Phillipe.

He darted in front of Papa and raced up to the stake on the bank. The rowboat, still flying the pirate flag, bobbed gently on the water. Beside it was a small, red canoe. It was beautiful.

When he looked more carefully, Phillipe saw that the varnish had been worn off the paddlers' seats and the canvas sides had been patched in two or three places. The new red paint did not quite match the original color. The paddles had knicks along the bottom of the blades. But it was beautiful.

"Is it ours?" asked Armand.

"Oui," answered Papa. "I bought it from Tom Straight Arrow."

"Can we go for a ride in it?" Albertine asked.

"Oui," said Papa.

"Oh, Gabriel, is it safe?" asked Mama.

"Now, Mama, even if they tip over the water's less than a foot deep."

"But I don't want them to fall in the cold water."

"They won't. Not when I teach them how to be safe. After all, they're Doucets, aren't they?" He pulled the canoe close to the bank and climbed into the stern. "Do you want the first ride, Mama?" he asked.

Mama backed away. "Non! Not at all. I have work to do. Come, Louise."

Papa and Emmanuel took the first turn to show how

it was done. They were both good paddlers and the children watched in delight as the red canoe moved swiftly upstream. As they turned, some gulls swooped down and flew beside the canoe, which easily kept up to them.

Phillipe whooped. "It's so fast!" he said.

"Like flying," said Celine.

Manny went to chop wood for Mama. Papa showed the twins how to climb in without tipping the canoe and then took them for a ride. They were too small to paddle and they soon got tired of sitting absolutely still on the hard bottom of the canoe. They left to play somewhere else. Phillipe and Celine loved the canoe. Papa spent the morning teaching them to paddle. By noon, he allowed then to go out alone, Phillipe in the stern and Celine in the prow while he watched from shore. Sometimes the two paddles weren't in rhythm, sometimes one of them missed a stroke, sometimes Phillipe steered them in to the bank. Papa said all they needed was practise.

As soon as dinner and the afternoon chores were finished, they were afloat again. As well as the stream that flowed through their property, there were many little rivulets which drained into it. Some of them opened into ponds. Celine and Phillipe spent a happy afternoon exploring them. They saw frogs, turtles and water beetles skittering over the surface of the water. While they were paddling quietly away from the nest of an nervous black tern, Celine said, "Papa gave us a good surprise."

"Yes," answered Phillipe. "We could have a real adventure in this canoe. We could be pirates looking for a place to hide our treasure."

"Not pirates," said Celine. "Not in a canoe. Explorers, maybe, or voyageurs."

"Oui! Oui!" agreed Phillipe. "Voyageurs, like great great great great great grandpère."

"Too many greats," laughed Celine.

The Doucet family had always been in the fur trade. Grandpère's grandfather was a Canadien who helped to paddle huge freight canoes between Fort William and the trading posts on the Saskatchewan River for the Hudson Bay Company. His sons were also voyageurs and trappers. Grandpère was the first of his family to be a full-time farmer, but he ran a trapline in the winter, just as Papa did. Phillipe and Celine had heard many stories about the early fur traders.

They decided to ask Mama if they could pack a lunch and go exploring the next day. That would fill in a day before school opened.

CHAPTER THREE

Next morning the whole family watched as Celine and Phillipe set off on their voyage of exploration. The paddlers were wearing woollen touques and had wrapped long scarves around their waists in imitation of a voyageur's ceinture or sash. Phillipe had stuck one of Papa's old tobacco pipes in his sash because he knew that the voyageurs sometimes rested for as long as it took to smoke a pipe of tobacco. A canvas wrapped bundle of provisions lay squarely in the bottom of the canoe. In the old days it would have contained pemmican and a bottle of rum, not jam sandwiches and a sealer of water. A square of red flannel on a willow twig waved bravely behind Phillipe in the stern.

Mama wanted them to go upstream toward their grandparents' farm in case they got tired. Phillipe and Celine scorned that idea. They were explorers out to discover new lands. They turned west and headed towards Lake Manitoba, many miles away. It would take days to go that far.

"Be back for supper," called Mama.

Emmanuel waved his hands at the flat landscape. "Watch out for rapids," he teased.

"Bon voyage!" shouted Papa.

They paddled steadily until they had gone past the places they had explored the day before. Celine was glad to rest when Phillipe called a halt and pretended to smoke his pipe. She laid her paddle across the prow and looked back. They were truly in Unknown Territory. Although the trees were bare of leaves they were thick enough to screen a view of the home buildings. The vegetation was familiar and the same birds flew through the air, but there was no sign of human beings. Celine and Phillipe felt like real explorers.

Phillipe spotted a black and red water snake.

"I never saw one of those before," he said.

"Neither did I," said Celine. "We don't have that kind back home."

"I wonder what other strange things we'll find?" said Phillipe. "En avant!"

They were glad to be moving again because they left the mosquitoes behind. In a few minutes the stream divided into two branches to flow around a slight rise in the ground.

"Which way?" asked Celine.

Phillipe backpaddled gently to keep the canoe steady while he gazed around. Something was shimmering over the ground off to the right.

"Look, Celine. What's that?"

"I don't know. Let's find out."

They paddled slowly and quietly to the north. The water was now so shallow that the paddles touched bottom. Soon they were pushing the canoe through bright green reeds as high as their heads. And then they came to the shimmering cloud.

"Dragonflies," whispered Celine. "Dozens of them."

"Hundreds," breathed Phillipe in awe.

The sunlight shone on and through the transparent wings of two kinds of dragonflies. The bigger one was pale blue and the other had a green head and green and brown striped body. They were feasting on the mosquitoes as they hatched in the stagnant pool.

After watching in delight for a few minutes, Phillipe said, "I'm going to catch one."

Phillipe had been a champion grasshopper catcher since he was five years old. He just pounced on the bug with his cupped hands. That didn't work for butterflies. Once Mama had given him the frame and handle of an old sieve when the wire mesh wore out. Celine had helped him sew a cheesecloth bag onto the frame to make a butterfly net. He caught a few specimens with it. But no matter how hard he tried, he had never caught a dragonfly. Now was his chance. One of the blue ones settled on a reed just level with Phillipe's shoulder. He could see the lines on the four wings and the white tip of its tail.

He quietly slipped his paddle into the canoe. The dragonfly paid no intention to him. It was too intent on the insects flying just above the surface of the water. It swayed closer on its reed.

"Keep us steady," Phillipe whispered to Celine.

She pushed her paddle down into the muddy bottom. Carefully she turned her head to watch Phillipe watching the dragonfly watching the mosquitoes. Suddenly, she saw something else. A big, brown leopard frog was hiding in a clump of duck weed almost under the dragonfly's perch. Only his head was sticking up. His yellow rimmed eyes were staring at the dragonfly. Just as his tongue darted out, Celine slapped the water with the side of her paddle. The dragonfly flew away, the mosquitoes disappeared and the frog sank into the mud.

Phillipe yelled, "What did you do that for?"

"The frog was going to eat him," said Celine. "And he's so pretty. Anyway, explorers don't stop to catch insects."

"There's nothing to explore in here," said Phillipe. "Let's go back and try the other way."

As they turned the canoe, a family of muskrats slipped noiselessly into the water.

Phillipe grinned. "They know we're fur traders," he said.

The south bank of the stream was covered with trees. There were a few spruce amid the bare aspen and poplars and some of the undergrowth was pale green. This stream was deeper than the first one they had tried. They paddled quickly and soon found themselves surrounded by woods on both sides.

Phillipe was aware of a sound he couldn't quite place.

"Listen, Celine, do you hear that?"

"What?"

"That sound."

"Oui, I hear it. It's like when Mama swishes the water in the wash tub."

"Oui! That's it!" shouted Phillipe. "It's running water. The river must be just behind those trees."

"What river?"

"The river that goes to the lake. This stream will run into it soon. We'll be on our way to the lake."

Phillipe knew that the lake was very far away and he knew that there were no pirates any more. But wouldn't it be exciting if around the next bend they came to the mouth of the stream? Then out on the wide river they could see all the way to the lake? And on the lake there was a pirate boat? He imagined it with its sails full of wind and the skull and crossbones fluttering from the highest mast.

CHAPTER FOUR

While Phillipe dreamed of his pirate ship, Celine noticed that the stream was widening into a pond. Soon she saw the reason why.

Beavers had built a dam across the stream. One of them was gnawing at a slender birch right now. When it saw the canoe, it waddled to the pool, slapped its tail on the water and disappeared.

The sound woke Phillipe from his dream.

"Oh, no!" he groaned. "How can we get to the river? I know. We'll portage."

"Around the dam, you mean?" asked Celine doubtfully.

She liked the idea of portaging. That would make them real voyageurs. But she couldn't see any dry land near the dam.

"No, I guess not," said Phillipe. "Let's go back. We passed a little beach back there. I think there was a path, too. Maybe it's a trail to the river."

The beach was tiny, just big enough to pull up the canoe and stand beside it.

Phillipe pointed to the broken branches on the lower part of the trees.

"Somebody's been through here," he said.

"Indians, maybe," answered Celine. "Going to trap muskrats and beavers. But we're the first voyageurs."

"Oui," said Phillipe. "We'll find the Indians and trade with them. You take the pack. I'll carry the canoe."

They had seen pictures of voyageurs on a portage. Two men would carry the big canoe, turned upside down, on their shoulders. The other men would fasten ninety pound packs to their backs with a tump line across their foreheads.

After helping Phillipe to turn the canoe over, Celine took off her sash and tied it around the lunch parcel. She left a big enough loop to drape across her forehead and fastened it into place. As soon as she moved, the belt slipped down to her neck and the weight of the pack nearly choked her. After three tries she gave up and retied the sash around her waist with the pack dangling down her leg. She now had her arms free to carry the paddles.

Meanwhile, Phillipe was trying to hoist the canoe on to his shoulders. He crawled underneath on his hands and knees, twisted around so that he was facing the forward seat and then grasped the edges of the canoe and tried to lift it. It was too heavy. He wriggled forward. Maybe if he got one end up, he could shift it forward to balance the load. He did it! He was on his feet holding the prow of the canoe over his head. But the stern was still resting on the ground. He couldn't drag it through the woods that way and his arms and legs were already trembling with the strain.

"Celine," he called.

She peered under the canoe.

"What?"

"Lift the other end and help me get nearer the middle."

Celine tugged at the stern. The canoe that was as light as a bird in the water now felt far heavier than the biggest stone they had cleared from the field.

"I can't do it," she called.

Phillipe groaned.

"Come under here with me," he said.

She did.

"Now, move backwards until the canoe is on your back and then straighten up."

She did.

"Hey, we did it!" said Phillipe as the weight lessened on his arms and legs. "Now we can go. Ready? En avant! Right, left! Right, left!"

After a few steps, Celine said, "It's heavy."

"Sure it's heavy. But we voyageurs are strong."

"You haven't got a package bumping your leg," she muttered.

They struggled along the faint path for a few more steps. Then Celine called, "Phillipe!"

"What?"

"The paddles. We forgot the paddles."

Phillipe groaned again. This was not going to work. What was the use of carrying the canoe to the river if they didn't take the paddles? Grandpère had told him that voyageurs often made two or three trips over a portage until all the baggage was transported. But he didn't know how long this portage was. Would they have time for two trips? Would they be too tired to make a second trip? His arms already felt like limp rope.

"Put it down," he said.

"How?" asked Celine.

That was a good question. The path was very narrow and there were sharp branches on either side. Away off here in the wilderness they must not injure either themselves or the canoe. Phillipe thought for a few more seconds.

"We'll kneel down," he said, "and then tilt it to the left. Lower it onto your head to keep it steady."

"Ouch, it hurts," said Celine.

"It's only for a few seconds," answered Phillipe. "Ready? Right knee first. Down. Now left knee. Down. Now tilt to the left. Left, I said! Whew!"

They crawled out from under the canoe. Celine rubbed her knees.

"There's stones here," she said.

"That's probably why the Indians made the path in this place. Good solid ground." He stared at the canoe sadly. "I really wanted to get to the river," he said.

Celine rubbed her aching arms.

"We'll never get it up again," she said.

"I know." Phillipe took off his touque and swished it angrily at the mosquitoes. "We might as well go home."

Celine stared into the bush. The path seemed slightly wider up ahead.

"It can't be very far," she said. "I can hear the river. If we turn the canoe right side up, we could carry it."

Phillipe shook his head.

"Sure we could," said Celine. "You get on one side and I'll take the other."

"We'd have to walk sideways."

"So?"

"That's not how the voyageurs did it. People will laugh at us."

Celine looked all around.

"Who's here to see?" she asked.

Phillipe grinned. "Vraiment," he said. "Let's do it."

He went back for the paddles. Celine untied the parcel from her waist. They placed both in the canoe.

With many stops to rest their arms and swat at mosquitoes, they finally reached a large, flat rock that sloped down to the river. Thankfully they put down the canoe and ran to the water's edge. It wasn't a very big river. At this point it was only twice as wide as their own stream, but the water was deep and it flowed swiftly. Phillipe threw a twig in to test the speed of the current.

"That will take us to the lake in no time," he said.

CHAPTER FIVE

"The lake's far away," said Celine. She didn't want to fight with Phillipe but she did want to take his mind off the lake. She said, "Let's eat. I'm starving."

"Me, too," said Phillipe.

It was easy to pretend that they were explorers eating pemmican by a river they had discovered There were no signs of human life anywhere. No birds sang. No animals called. The only sound was the gurgling of the river.

They were quiet, each lost in a private dream. Celine was presenting the Governor of the Company with a map of the new territory and receiving a medal in exchange. Phillipe was paddling a canoe laden with furs out to a boat on the lake. It look surprisingly like a pirate ship.

They were startled back to reality by the sound of breaking branches upstream. They stared across the river. What was there? Indians? Rival traders?

"Something big, that's for sure," whispered Phillipe.

In a moment a huge moose stepped out of the bush. He stood with his front feet in the water as he swung his head from side to side sniffing the air. Then he slid into the river and swam toward their side.

In a few minutes he climbed out on the rock only yards away from them. Celine held her breath and shrank back. When he shook himself, drops of water hit her. She wrinkled her nose against the rank smell of wet fur. The moose stared at the humans for a few moments then it stepped around the canoe and disappeared down the path.

Celine let out a long breath of relief.

Phillipe was excited. "I'll bet that path was made by the moose, not the Indians," he said. "We are the first people to find this river. Let's see where it goes."

It was easy paddling on the river. The canoe sped along like a real fur trade canoe. Soon they were singing one of the voyageur songs that Mama had learned to play on the harmonium.

Celine broke off in the middle of a line. "Phillipe," she screamed. "Rapids! Rapids ahead!"

She lifted her paddle from the water. The river needed no help from her to sweep them over the crest. Before she could see how deep the fall was, the canoe was bobbing and weaving over the rocks. In fact the drop was only two feet and the slope was gradual. Phillipe steered them safely through.

"Wow! That was fun!" he yelled.

"Oui," answered Celine, not quite so enthusiastically. "You're a good canoe man, like all the Doucets."

"A good canoe man takes care of his boat. We'd better check for leaks," said Phillipe.

They landed on a little beach at the base of a slight hill.

There were no holes in the canoe. Lifting her eyes

from examining the hull, Celine was startled to find a tall Indian watching them.

Her gasp made Phillipe jump up. Where had he come from? They had heard nothing, not even the big green canoe being dragged on to the beach.

"You must be the Doucet kids," he said.

"How do you know?" asked Phillipe.

"That's my old canoe. I sold it to Doucet a couple of days ago. I'm Tom."

"I'm Phillipe and this is Celine. Papa let us have the canoe for an adventure."

Tom looked at their touques, woollen sashes and moccasins. "Voyageurs, eh? Where are you going?" he asked

"To the lake," answered Phillipe.

"Not to the lake," said Celine quickly. "It's too far."

"Much too far," agreed Tom. "And too dangerous in that little canoe. The waves would swamp you."

Phillipe's shoulders slumped and the corners of his mouth turned down.

"I just wanted to see the lake," he said.

"You can do that," said Tom. "Come."

Three long strides took him into the woods. Phillipe and Celine ran to keep up with him. For several minutes they climbed the hill. When they paused in a small clearing at the top, they could see trees and the river and more high ground.

"Are there lots of Indians around here?" asked Celine.

"Used to be," said Tom.

Celine whispered to Phillipe. "Good place for a fur trade post."

Phillipe nodded.

"Where's the lake?" he asked Tom.

Tom pointed to a higher hill to the north and started off again.

Phillipe's mind was hurrying as fast as his legs. He was going to see the lake. Of course, there wouldn't be a pirate ship but there might be fishing boats. Maybe a whole fleet of them.

Neither Phillipe nor Celine was used to climbing and they were panting heavily when they joined Tom at the top. He pointed west.

"There it is. Lake Manitoba."

CHAPTER SIX

It took several seconds for Phillipe to see the lake. He looked past miles and miles of woodland dotted with smaller lakes and streams. And it was hard to tell the lake from the sky. But at last his eyes adjusted and he could see the huge expanse of water.

"It goes on forever," said Celine, in awe.

"It's big," agreed Tom.

"And empty," replied Celine.

There wasn't even a dot on the water that Phillipe's imagination could make into a pirate boat, but he wasn't disappointed. The lake was magnificent. There was plenty of room for a great battle between pirate ships and merchantmen.

When they got back to the canoes, Tom said he would travel with them and lead the way up the rapids.

"There's an easy way to get through," he said, "but you have to know where it is."

It certainly looked easy for Tom in his big green canoe, but Celine and Phillipe had to work hard to paddle against the current and then climb the rapids.

Once up, Celine rested her paddle across the prow and took deep breaths.

"Hey!" yelled Phillipe. "Keep paddling! We're going backwards!"

Tom was waiting at the place where they'd had

lunch. Phillipe hoped that he would leave them before he saw how they carried the canoe over the portage. It would be too humiliating to be seen staggering sideways.

Instead, with one easy motion, Tom grasped the sides of the red canoe, swung it up over his head and loped down the path. Phillipe followed with the paddles and Celine carried the empty lunch bag. Imitating Tom's stride, they crossed the portage like real voyageurs.

Tom said goodbye at the stream that would take them home.

The paddling was easy again. They could dream as they drifted along. Celine turned and grinned at her brother.

"We had a successful expedition," she said.

"Oui. We discovered a lake and a river that flows into it," he answered.

"And a good place for a trading post," she said. "On high ground so it won't flood. Lots of logs to build a fort and feed the fires."

Phillipe added, "Lots of furs, too. Muskrat and beaver."

"And a food supply for the men."

"Oui. Moose and ducks."

"And friendly Indians."

Phillipe dug deep with his paddle and the canoe shot forward. "The Company will be pleased with our report," he said.

Ten minutes later they saw the buildings of their

home away off in the distance. Soon they were close enough to see someone standing by the stream. The figure turned and ran.

"That's Armand," laughed Phillipe.

"Gone to tell the others we're coming," said Celine.

They grinned as they watched the family come from all directions to stand beside the stake. They were all there: Papa, Mama, Robert, Louisa, Armand and Albertine and Emmanuel. Celine and Phillipe couldn't wait to tell about their great adventure.

"Allo! Allo!" they yelled.

"We ran the rapids!"

"We saw the lake!"

"We met Tom!"

"We portaged!"

Celine's shout trailed off. She had caught sight of another person with the family. He was a skinny man wearing a white shirt and black pants tucked into high boots.

"It must be the teacher," she said.

"Look!" said Phillipe. "He has an eye patch. He's a pirate! I knew it! M. Henri Lafitte is a pirate."

Constance Horne was born in Winnipeg. She taught high school in Minnedosa, Manitoba, Nelson and Vancouver, B.C. Her other children's titles include: *The Accidental Orphan* (1998), *Emily Carr's Woo* (1995), *Trapped by Coal* (1994), *The Jo Boy Deserts and Other Stories* (1992), and *Nykola and Granny Gage* (1989). Married with four grown children and two grandsons, she now lives in Victoria.

Mia Hansen was born in 1970 in the town of Ayr, Ontario, where she pursued illustration, cartooning, and dollmaking. At the age of 19, she wrote and illustrated the picture book *Binky Bemelman and the Big City Begonia*. From there, Mia went on to study Fine Arts at the University of Guelph. She now resides in Vancouver, British Columbia. Along with illustration, her work includes graphic design, painting, silkscreened clothing, and hand-painted wall dolls.

If you liked this book...
you might enjoy these other Hodgepog Books:
for grades 5–8

Into the Sun
by Luanne Armstrong, illustrated by Robin LeDrew
ISBN 0-9686899-9-X $8.95

Cross My Heart
by Janet Miller, illustrated by Martin Rose
ISBN 0-9730831-0-7 $8.95

And to read yourself in grades 3–5
or to read to younger kids.

Ben and the Carrot Predicament
by Mar'ce Merrell, illustrated by Barbara Hartmann
ISBN 1-895836-54-9 $4.95

Getting Rid of Mr. Ributus
by Alison Lohans, illustrated by Barbara Hartmann
ISBN 1-895836-53-0 $6.95

A Real Farm Girl
By Susan Ioannou, illustrated by James Rozak
ISBN 1-895836-52-2 $6.95

A Gift for Johnny Know-It-All
by Mary Woodbury, illustrated by Barbara Hartmann
ISBN 1-895836-27-1 $5.95

Mill Creek Kids
by Colleen Heffernan, illustrated by Sonja Zacharias
ISBN 1-895836-40-9 $5.95

Arly & Spike
by Luanne Armstrong, illustrated by Chao Yu
ISBN 1-895836-37-9 $4.95

A Friend for Mr. Granville
by Gillian Richardson, illustrated by Claudette Maclean
ISBN 1-895836-38-7 $5.95

Maggie & Shine
by Luanne Armstrong, illustrated by Dorothy Woodend
ISBN 1-895836-67-0 $6.95

Butterfly Gardens
by Judith Benson, illustrated by Lori McGregor McCrae
ISBN 1-895836-71-9 $5.95

The Duet
by Brenda Silsbe, illustrated by Gaelin Akin
ISBN 0-9686899-1-4 $5.95

Jeremy's Christmas Wish
by Glen Huser, illustrated by Martin Rose
ISBN 0-9686899-2-2 $5.95

Let's Wrestle
by Lyle Weis, illustrated by Will Milner and Nat Morris
ISBN 0-9686899-4-9 $5.95

A Pocketful of Rocks
by Deb Loughead, illustrated by Avril Woodend
ISBN 0-9686899-7-3 $5.95

Logan's Lake
by Margriet Ruurs, illustrated by Robin LeDrew
ISBN 1-9686899-8-1 $5.95

Fuzzy Wuzzy
by Norma Charles, illustrated by Galan Akin
ISBN 0-9730831- 2-3 $6.95

And for readers in grade 1-2, or to read to pre-schoolers

Sebastian's Promise
by Gwen Molnar, illustrated by Kendra McCleskey
ISBN 1-895836-65-4 $4.95

Summer With Sebastian
by Gwen Molnar, illustrated by Kendra McClesky
ISBN 1-895836-39-5 $4.95

The Noise in Grandma's Attic
by Judith Benson, illustrated by Shane Hill
ISBN 1-895836-55-7 $4.95

Pet Fair
by Deb Loughead, illustrated by Lisa Birke
ISBN 0-9686899-3-0 $5.95